COLORING BOOK

for

Stories of the Prophets in the Holy Qur'an

May the peace and blessings of Allah be upon them

SHAHADA SHARELLE ABDUL HAQQ

TUGHRA
BOOKS

New Jersey

Published by Tughra Books
335 Clifton Ave.
Clifton, NJ, 07011, USA
www.tughrabooks.com

ISBN: 978-1-59784-940-1

In the Name of Allah, the All-Merciful, the All-Compassionate

TABLE OF CONTENTS

Prophet Adam, the Father of Humankind   7

Prophet Enoch (Idris), a Prophet Raised to a High Rank   11

Prophet Noah (Nuh) and the Great Flood   13

Prophet Hud and the Storm   17

Prophet Salih and the Camel   21

Prophet Abraham (Ibrahim), the Friend of Allah   25

Prophet Ishmael (Ismail) and the Sacrifice   30

Prophet Lot (Lut) and the People of Sodom   34

Prophet Isaac (Ishaq), the Son Heralded by Angels   39

Prophet Jacob (Yaqup), the Wise Father   40

Prophet Joseph (Yusuf), the Forgiving   44

Prophet Shuaib, the Orator   48

Prophet Job (Ayyub), Who Endured   51

Prophet Moses (Musa) and the Pharaoh   55

Prophet Aaron (Harun), the Eloquent   59

Prophet Ezekiel (Dhu'l-Kifl), a Prophet of Fortitude   61

Prophet David (Dawud), the Valiant   63

Prophet Solomon (Sulaiman), the Gifted   66

Prophet Elijah (Ilyas), a Messenger of Allah   70

Prophet Elisha (Al-Yasa) A Believing Servant of Allah   72

Prophet Jonah (Yunus), the Repentant   74

Prophet Zachariah (Zakariya), the Worshipper   79

Prophet John (Yahya), the Forebearing   83

Prophet Jesus (Isa), the Healer   87

Prophet Muhammad, the Seal of the Prophets   91

Prophet Adam

The Father of Humankind

Prophet Adam (pbuh), the Father of Humankind, was taught the names of everything.
Prophet Adam (pbuh) and his wife lived in a garden and ate the fruits there.

Allah (SWT) forbade them to eat from one tree. However, Iblis (Satan) tempted Adam and his wife to eat from the forbidden tree. They disobeyed Allah (SWT).

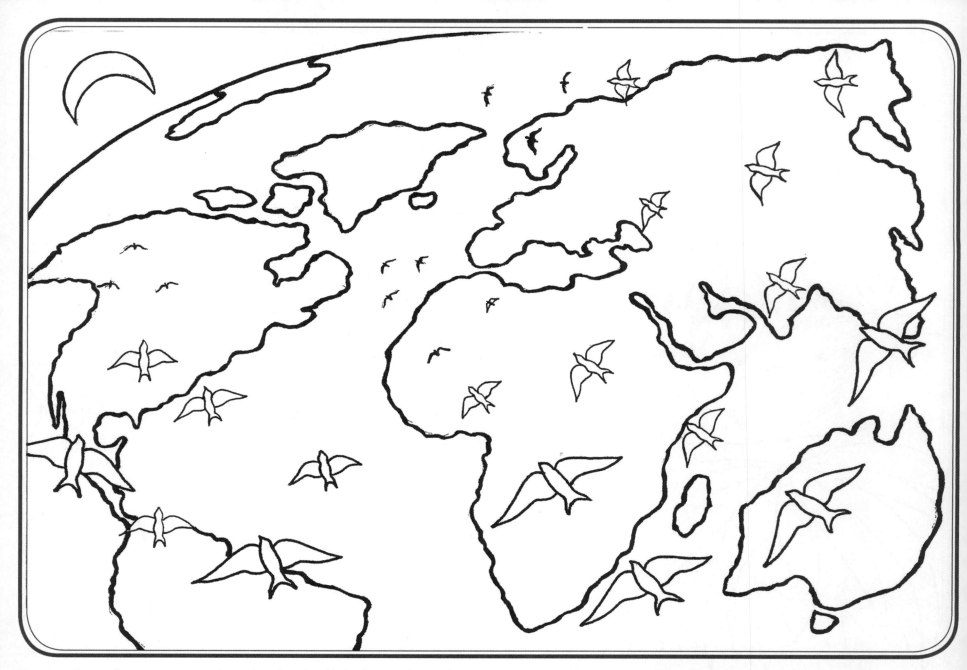

10 But they repented and asked Allah (SWT) to forgive them. Allah (SWT) forgave them and made them leave the garden to live on Earth.

Prophet Enoch (Idris)

A Prophet Raised to a High Rank

Idris

Enoch

ادريس

12   Prophet Idris (pbuh) was a man of truth and sincerity. Allah (SWT) raised him to a high status.

Prophet Noah (Nuh)

and the Great Flood

14   Prophet Noah (pbuh) called his people to worship Allah (SWT) for nine hundred and fifty years, but most of them would not listen.

Allah (SWT) told Prophet Noah (pbuh) to build an ark and to place two of every kind of animal, male and female, in it.

15

16 Only a few people worshipped Allah (SWT) while the rest laughed at Prophet Noah (pbuh). The flood drowned all of those that did not board the ark.

Prophet Hud

and the Storm

18 Prophet Hud (pbuh) lived among the People of *Ad*. These people worshipped other gods besides Allah (SWT).

Prophet Hud (pbuh) asked the people to obey Allah (SWT) or they would be punished.

The People of Ad refused to obey the Prophet and were thus destroyed by a sand storm.

Prophet Salih

and the Camel

عَلَيْهِ السَّلَام

22 Prophet Salih (pbuh) lived among the People of Thamud. These strong people carved houses out of the mountain.

The Thamud people asked Prophet Salih (pbuh) to make Allah (SWT) cause a pregnant female camel to appear from the mountain.

Allah (SWT) sent a beautiful pregnant camel, but later they killed her.
Allah (SWT) destroyed the Thamud people with an earthquake.

Prophet Abraham (Ibrahim)

The Friend of Allah

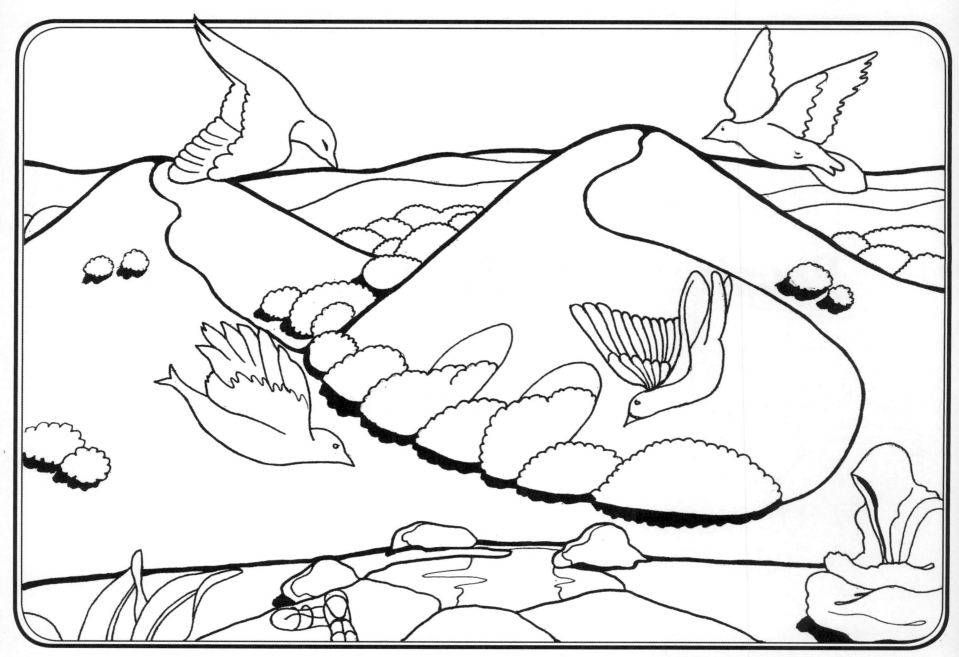

Prophet Abraham (pbuh), the father of many nations, is the friend of Allah (SWT).

Prophet Abraham (pbuh) was very sad as a young boy to know his father made sculptures of idol gods. 27

28   One day, Prophet Abraham (pbuh) destroyed these idols and told the people to ask the large idol to speak and prove that it had powers. But, of course, it could not.

29

Prophet Ishmael (Ismail)

and the Sacrifice

Prophet Ishmael (pbuh) was the first born son of Prophet Abraham (pbuh), and his wife, Hagar.

Prophet Abraham (pbuh) had a vision from Allah (SWT) to sacrifice Ishmael (pbuh).

Both Prophet Abraham (pbuh) and Ishmael (pbuh) were obedient servants to Allah (SWT) so Allah saved Ishmael (pbuh) and a ram was sacrificed instead.

33

Prophet Lot (Lut)

and the People of Sodom

Prophet Lot (pbuh) lived in the city of Sodom where men did evil to other men, and stole from travelers, and killed them.

Three angels in the form of men became the guests of Prophet Lot (pbuh).

The Angel Jibreel told Prophet Lot (pbuh) that the evil people of Sodom, including Prophet Lot's (pbuh) wife, would be destroyed.

Prophet Isaac (Ishaq)

The Son Heralded by the Angels

Angels came to Prophet Abraham (pbuh) and Sarah in their old age. They gave the good news that they were going to have a son, named Isaac. Prophet Isaac (pbuh) was one of the best men.

Prophet Jacob (Yaqup)

The Wise Father

Prophet Jacob (pbuh) gathered his 12 sons around him at the end of his life and asked his sons, "Who will you worship after I am dead?"

42   The faithful sons said they would worship the one true God (Allah SWT), not any false god.

Prophet Joseph (Yusuf)

The Forgiving

As a young boy, Joseph told his father he saw in his dream eleven stars, the sun, and the moon bow before him.

His brothers were very jealous of Prophet Joseph (pbuh). They threw him in a well.

Prophet Joseph (pbuh) became the Minister of Finance of Egypt. His family were in awe of his status and showed him great respect.

Prophet Shuaib

The Orator

The Madyan people were merchants who cheated people in the marketplace. Prophet Shuaib called on his people to believe in one God and to stop cheating. 49

Allah (SWT) caused the disbelieving people of Madyan to become buried in an earthquake.

Prophet Job (Ayyub)

Who Endured

52   Prophet Job (pbuh) sincerely worshipped Allah (SWT). He was healthy, wealthy and with children.

To test Prophet Job's (pbuh) sincerity, Allah (SWT) took everything away from him and afflicted him with disease. He suffered for a long time but never complained and asked Allah's (SWT) mercy.

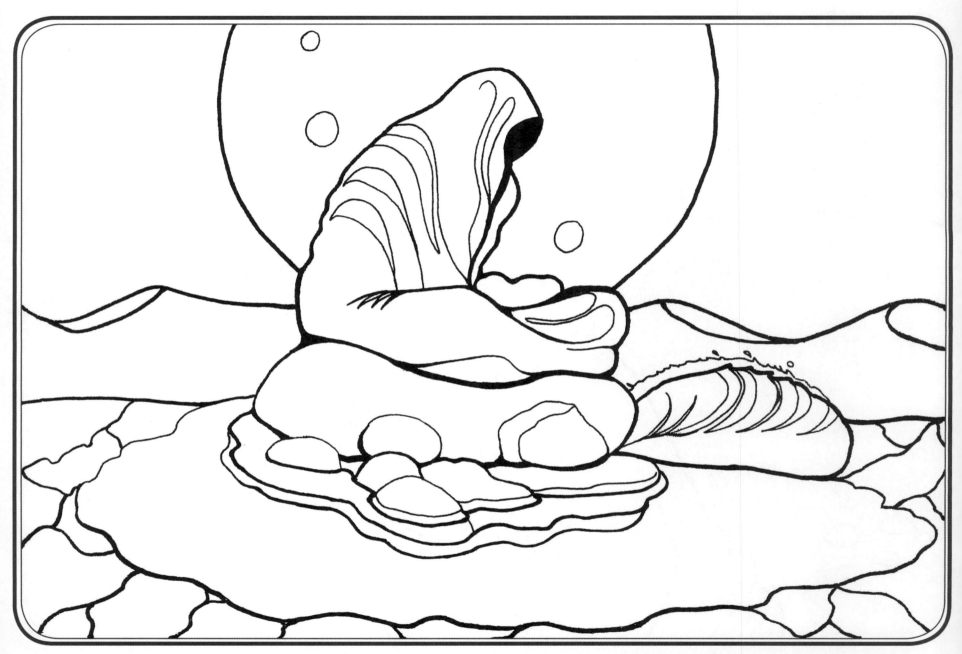

54   Allah (SWT) told him to strike the ground with his foot wherefrom a spring of water came, which healed him. Allah (SWT) returned his wealth to him as well.

Prophet Moses (Musa)

and the Pharaoh

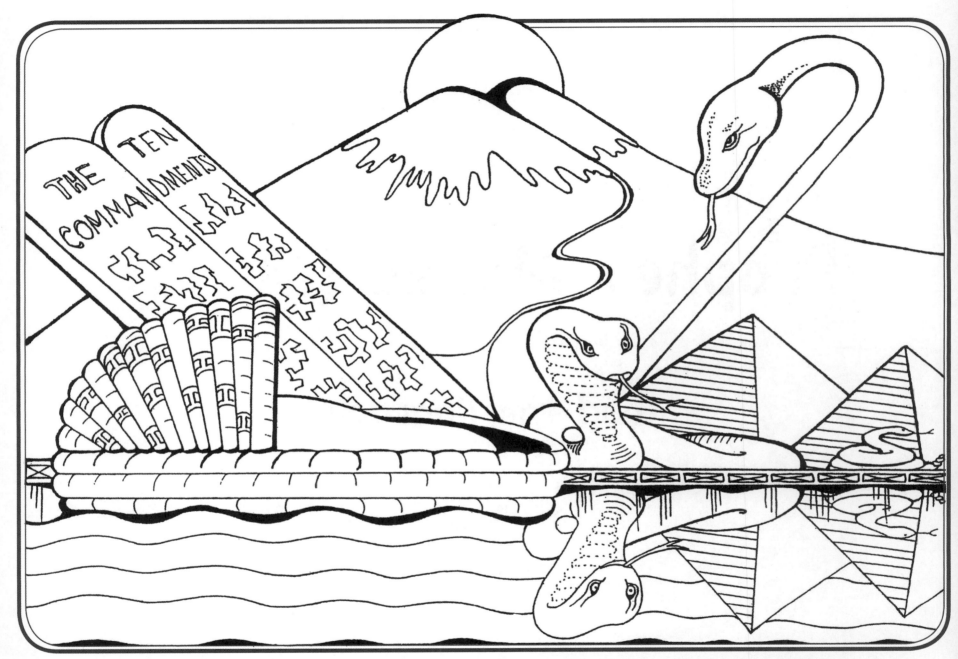

Prophet Moses (pbuh) was born an Israelite boy during the rule of an evil Egyptian Pharaoh.

Prophet Moses (pbuh) challenged Pharaoh. Allah (SWT) gave him miracles. His staff became a snake and ate the snakes of the Pharaoh's magicians.

58 Pharaoh became angry and his stubborn disbelief and oppression of the people of Egypt caused Allah (SWT) to bring a plague of frogs and locusts.

Prophet Aaron (Harun)

The Eloquent

60   Prophet Aaron (pbuh), the brother of Prophet Moses (pbuh), struggled with the Israeli people as they
made a golden calf to worship.

Prophet Ezekiel (Dhu'l-Kifl)

A Prophet of Fortitude

Dhul Kifl
Ezekiel

نور الكفل

Prophet Ezekiel (pbuh) was a righteous man, one of faithfulness and patience.

Prophet David (Dawud)

The Valiant

64   Prophet David (pbuh), a shepherd boy, used his sling shot to kill a lion and a bear
to protect his father's sheep.

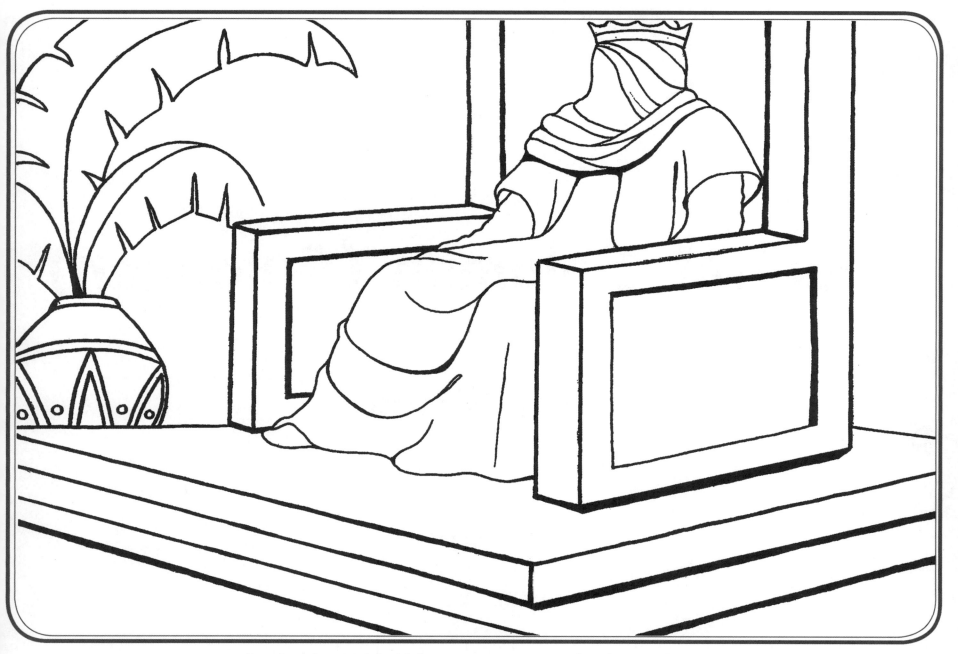

Prophet David (pbuh) became a strong and righteous king.

Prophet Solomon (Sulaiman)

The Gifted

السَّلَام عَلَيْهِ

Prophet Solomon (pbuh) inherited the kingdom of his father. He was given the gift of good judgment by saving a baby and his mother from injustice.

One day, Prophet Solomon's (pbuh) army was passing through a valley of ants.

The lead ant warned the others, so Prophet Solomon's (pbuh) army would not crush them.
Prophet Solomon (pbuh) heard them and did not harm the ants.

Prophet Elijah (Ilias)

A Messenger of Allah

Prophet Elijah (pbuh) called his people to fear Allah (SWT) because he was a devout servant.

Prophet Elisha (Al-Yasa)

A Believing Servant of God

Al-Yasa
Elisha
الیاس

Allah (SWT) chose Prophet Elisha (pbuh) and showed him the straight way.

73

Prophet Jonah (Yunus)

The Repentant

The people of Nineveh worshipped idols. Prophet Jonah (pbuh) was sent to teach them to worship Allah (SWT) alone. But they were not listening.

76 Prophet Jonah (pbuh) thought Allah (SWT) was going to punish this disobedient people. He left the city and boarded a boat. A terrible storm came and he was thrown overboard to be swallowed by a big fish.

The Prophet asked for Allah's (SWT) forgiveness. Allah forgave him, and the people of Nineveh from then on worshipped Allah (SWT) alone.

77

start

Finish

Prophet Zachariah (Zakariya)

The Worshipper

80   Prophet Zachariah (pbuh) spent his entire life in the service of Allah (SWT). He was now ninety years old.

One day he visited his niece Mary (Maryam) and saw fresh, but off-season fruit in her room. Maryam told her uncle that Allah (SWT) provides to whom He wills.

82 Prophet Zachariah (pbuh) asked from Allah (SWT) a son. Allah (SWT) blessed him and his aged wife with Prophet Yahya (pbuh).

Prophet John (Yahya)

The Forebearing

السَّلَامُ عَلَيْهِ

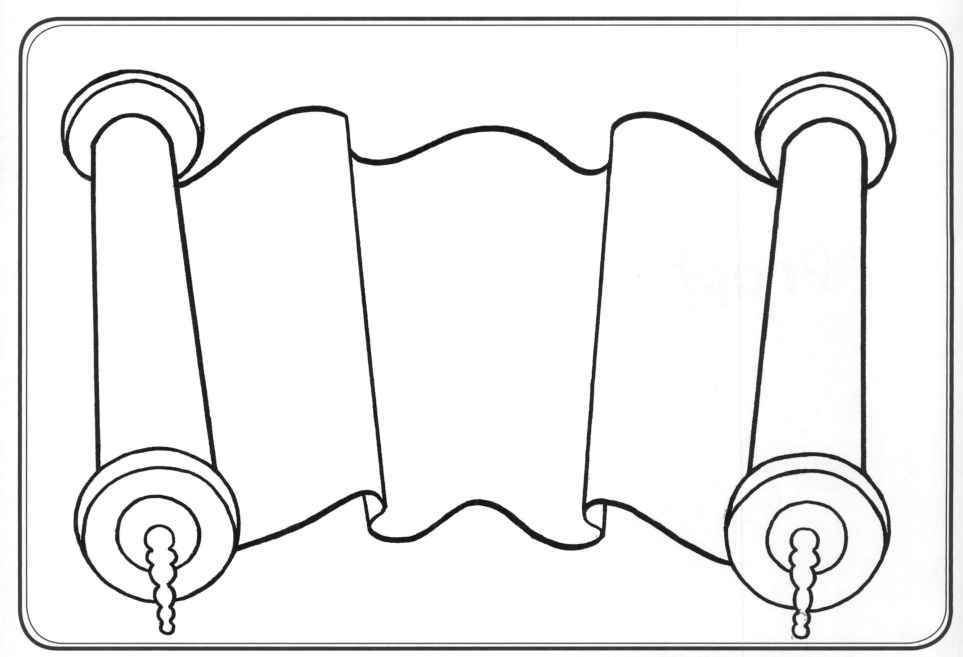

Prophet John (pbuh), the most knowledgeable man of his time, guarded the Holy Torah.
He told the people it was forbidden to mary one's niece.

Salome caused her uncle King Herod to fall in love with her and then asked the King to kill Prophet John (pbuh).

86   Salome and King Herod married after the death of Prophet John (pbuh) and Allah (SWT) did not let them live happily ever after.

Prophet Jesus (Isa)

The Healer

Mary (Maryam), the purest woman in the world, gave birth to
Prophet Jesus (pbuh) without a father.

Prophet Jesus (pbuh) was given the ability from Allah (SWT) to make the blind see and bring the dead to life.

Prophet Jesus (pbuh) was taken to heavens to the abode of Allah (SWT).

Prophet Muhammad

The Seal

Prophet Muhammad (pbuh) is the seal of Prophethood. That is, he was the last Prophet to come to humankind. His father died before he was born.

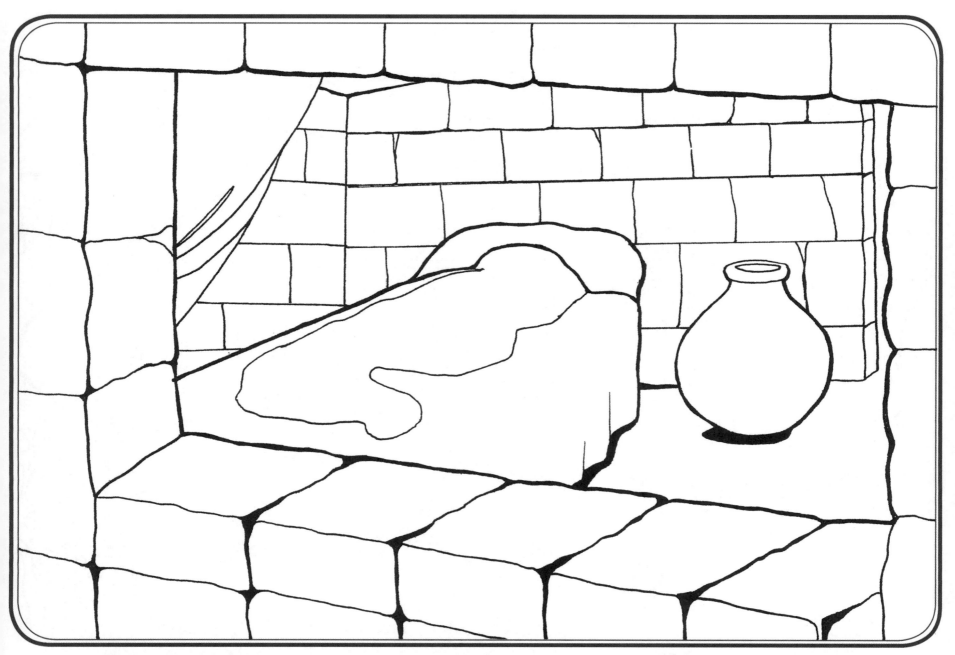

The Angel Gabriel (Gibreel) told the Prophet not to sleep in his bed, so the Prophet asked his nephew Ali to take his place. No harm came to him.

Allah (SWT) caused a spider web and a bird nest to form over the entrance of a cave to protect Prophet Muhammad (pbuh) and his companion Abu Bakr from enemies who wanted to kill them.

1. Sulaiman (pbuh)

2. Muhammad (pbuh)

3. Jonah (pbuh)

4. Noah (pbuh)

5. Adam (pbuh)

6. Shuaib (pbuh)

7. Hud (pbuh)

Match the titles to the Prophets

1. Zakariyya - Zachariah (pbuh)   Friend of Allah

2. Muhammad (pbuh)   The Healer

3. Ibrahim - Abraham (pbuh)   The Repentant

4. Yunus - Jonah (pbuh)   The Forebearing

5. Isa - Jesus (pbuh)   The Worshipper

6. Yahya - John (pbuh)   The Seal

Find the names of the Prophets in the word puzzle

S	H	U	A	I	B	Z	I	X	A	D	A	M
Y	N	U	S	S	M	H	D	J	E	S	U	S
A	E	L	H	Q	O	U	R	M	U	S	A	Y
Z	L	D	A	W	U	D	I	U	W	U	D	A
N	I	Y	R	I	A	B	S	H	Y	V	A	Q
O	A	U	U	E	M	C	R	A	J	X	M	U
A	S	N	N	F	D	A	Y	M	Y	O	Z	B
H	U	U	U	G	H	Y	N	M	U	Y	B	T
J	H	S	I	L	I	A	S	A	N	A	U	J
L	U	M	E	R	O	S	Q	D	U	H	I	B
Y	L	I	A	I	N	P	A	O	S	Y	K	L
K	K	K	U	I	S	M	A	I	L	A	N	M
I	A	L	Y	A	S	A	S	I	S	H	A	Q
Z	I	B	R	A	H	I	M	S	A	L	E	H

1. Father of Humankind	Harun - Aaron (pbuh)
2. The Challenged the Pharaoh	Ayyub - Job (pbuh)
3. Prophet of Madyan	Sulaiman - Solomon (pbuh)
4. The Wise Father	Yaqub - Jacob (pbuh)
5. The Valiant	Dawud - David (pbuh)
6. The Forgiving	Adam (pbuh)
7. Who Endured	Yusuf - Joseph (pbuh)
8. The Eloquent	Musa - Moses (pbuh)
9. The Gifted	Shuaib (pbuh)